How Much Is That Doggie in the Window?

SCHOLASTIC INC.

New York Toronto London Auckland Sydney
Mexico City New Delhi Hong Kong

How Much Is That Doggie in the Window?

Words and Music by **Bob Merrill**

As retold and illustrated by

IZA TRAPANI

ISBN 0-439-24942-2

"(How Much Is) That Doggie In The Window," words and music copyright © 1953 by Bob Merrill,
renewed 1981 by Golden Bell Songs.
Adaptation and illustrations copyright © 1997 by Iza Trapani.
All rights reserved.
Published by Scholastic Inc., 555 Broadway, New York, NY 10012,
by arrangement with Whispering Coyote Press.
SCHOLASTIC and associated logos are trademarks and/or registered
trademarks of Scholastic Inc.

12 11 10 9 8 7 6 5 4 3 2 1   1 2 3 4 5 6/0 09

Printed in the U.S.A.

First Scholastic printing, February 2001

Book design by *The Kids at Our House*
Text set in 22-point Goudy Old Style Bold

For Maciek and Kuba
with love
—I.T.

How much is that doggie in the window?
The one with the waggely tail.
How much is that doggie in the window?
I do hope that doggie's for sale.

That doggie's on sale for sixty dollars.
I'd even take five dollars off.
But you only have eleven fifty
I'm sorry, but that's not enough.

Perhaps you would rather buy a hamster,
A gerbil or maybe some mice?
These lizards and snakes are simply splendid.
I'll take fifty cents off the price.

Oh no mister, no, I want that doggie
Just look how he's wagging at me.
I'll go find a way to make some money
And I'll buy him, just wait and see.

I thought I'd sell lemonade on Monday—
Now that's a good plan, don't you think?
But it rained all day and most of Tuesday
And no one came out for a drink.

On Wednesday and Thursday I felt lousy—
I had a bad cold in my head.
The weather was great, but I was achy
And had to spend two days in bed.

On Friday my little baby sister
Fell down and she banged up her knee.
I went out and bought her frozen yogurt
And she was as pleased as could be.

On Saturday Mom was in the garden—
A bee stung her right on the toe.
I went out and bought her chocolate candy.
It made her feel better, you know.

On Sunday my Daddy got allergic.
He sneezed and his eyes itched real bad.
I went out and bought a box of tissues
And spent almost all that I had.

So that's why I didn't earn a penny.
I guess that I'm plain out of luck.
Last Monday I had eleven fifty
And now I have less than a buck.

Oh, where is that doggie in the window?
Oh, where did that cute doggie go?
I know that I can't afford to buy him.
I just thought I'd come say, "Hello."

Some people stopped in and bought that doggie
For their very special young son.
They bought him the dog so they could thank him
For all the nice things he had done.

Can that be the doggie from the window?
I wonder can that really be?
Oh, what a surprise! I never figured
That lucky young boy would be me.

How Much is that Doggie in the Window?

How much is that dog - gie in the win - dow? The one with the
wag - gel - y tail. How much is that dog - gie in the
win - dow? I do hope that dog - gie's for sale.

2. That doggie's on sale for sixty dollars.
   I'd even take five dollars off.
   But you only have eleven fifty
   I'm sorry, but that's not enough.

3. Perhaps you would rather buy a hamster,
   A gerbil or maybe some mice?
   These lizards and snakes are simply splendid.
   I'll take fifty cents off the price.

4. Oh no mister, no, I want that doggie
   Just look how he's wagging at me.
   I'll go find a way to make some money
   And I'll buy him, just wait and see.

5. I thought I'd sell lemonade on Monday—
   Now that's a good plan, don't you think?
   But it rained all day and most of Tuesday
   And no one came out for a drink.

6. On Wednesday and Thursday I felt lousy—
   I had a bad cold in my head.
   The weather was great, but I was achy
   And had to spend two days in bed.

7. On Friday my little baby sister
   Fell down and she banged up her knee.
   I went out and bought her frozen yogurt
   And she was as pleased as could be.

8. On Saturday Mom was in the garden—
   A bee stung her right on the toe.
   I went out and bought her chocolate candy.
   It made her feel better, you know.

9. On Sunday my Daddy got allergic.
   He sneezed and his eyes itched real bad.
   I went out and bought a box of tissues
   And spent almost all that I had.

10. So that's why I didn't earn a penny.
    I guess that I'm plain out of luck.
    Last Monday I had eleven fifty
    And now I have less than a buck.

11. Oh, where is that doggie in the window?
    Oh, where did that cute doggie go?
    I know that I can't afford to buy him.
    I just thought I'd come say, "Hello."

12. Some people stopped in and bought that doggie
    For their very special young son.
    They bought him the dog so they could thank him
    For all the nice things he had done.

13. Can that be the doggie from the window?
    I wonder can that really be?
    Oh, what a surprise! I never figured
    That lucky young boy would be me.